Elliot's
EMERGENCY

To David and Ian

Published in Great Britain in 1999 by Madcap Books, André Deutsch Ltd,
76 Dean Street, London, W1V 5HA

Text and illustrations copyright © 1998 by Andrea Beck

Elliot Moose and the Elliot Moose character are trademarks of Andrea Beck

Published by permission of Kids Can Press Ltd., Toronto, Ontario, Canada

ISBN 0 233 99682 6

Printed in Hong Kong

Elliot's EMERGENCY

Written and Illustrated by
ANDREA BECK

MADCAP

Elliot Moose

woke up and leapt out of bed. What a glorious morning!
He pulled on his shirt and grabbed his bag.
Today was a special day, and he was ready.

Elliot was going exploring
with his best friend, Socks. They
planned to travel far into the big
house and be away overnight.

Elliot ran to get his sleeping bag. As he scooped it up,
his leg brushed the woodwork, and he felt a sharp tug.
He was caught on something!

Elliot gave his leg a shake.
Then he tried pulling,
but nothing happened.

Socks would be waiting. He had to go!

Finally, he yanked with all his might and came free. But as he flew backward, he heard a terrible ripping sound.

Elliot looked down in horror.

"Socks!" he shrieked.

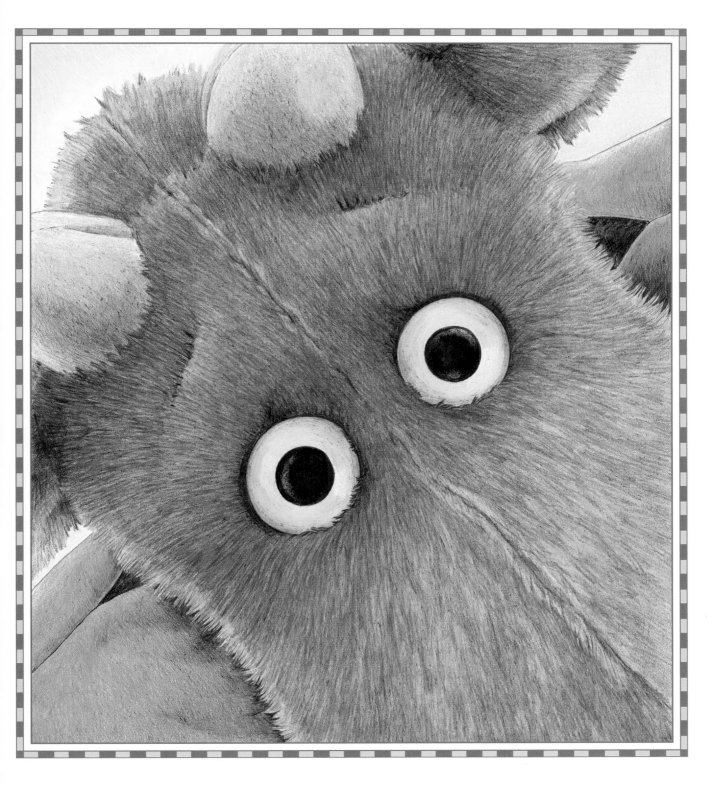

Socks raced over.
She gasped. Elliot's fuzzy leg was open!
"Are you okay?" she asked.
"No," whimpered Elliot.

Socks peered at the hole.
"Let's see if you can walk,"
she suggested.

Elliot bravely tried a few steps.
He didn't feel any different — a bit
drafty perhaps. But when he looked
down, he could see his stuffing.
What if it all came out?
For a moment he imagined himself as just an
empty shell of fur.

Frantically, Elliot rummaged through his things.

"Thank goodness!" he said, holding up a shiny pin. "Now everything will be fine."

Socks gently put the pin in place. But when she was done, there was still a little hole at each end of the tear.

Elliot tried walking again. Then he noticed a long thread dangling from his leg. And one of the little holes was getting bigger.

"Socks!" he cried. "I'm coming undone! Get help!"

Socks scrambled upstairs.
"Emergency!" she yelled.
"Elliot's coming apart!"
Lionel was the first one down.
He took a look and smiled.
"Nothing to worry about,"
he said. "We'll fix you up in no time.
I've been saving this tape. It'll do the trick." He
began to wrap it around Elliot's leg.
Elliot sighed with relief.
But the tape was old and the ends came unstuck.
Even worse, it took out some of Elliot's precious stuffing.
"Oh dear," fretted Lionel, "that wasn't very useful."
"No," said Elliot softly.

"Wait for us! We know what to
do in emergencies!"
called Paisley Bear and Amy
as they tumbled down the stairs.
They quickly examined
Elliot's leg.
"You need bandaging," they decided. "That's the answer."
But their small roll of bandage wrapped only one hole.
The other hole was getting bigger.
"Sorry, Elliot," said Paisley, "I thought we had more."
"Thanks anyway," said Elliot sadly.

"Our turn! Our turn!" cried Snowy and Puff. "We know what to do! We'll glue Elliot's leg!"

But when they'd finished, the hole slowly opened up again. Globs of sticky glue were everywhere.

Elliot fought back tears.

"It seemed like a good idea," he told the cubs. "Thanks for trying."

"Hang on, Elliot!" Angel stepped
forward. "I have just what you
need." She held up a large clip.
"This will hold your leg
together until the glue dries,"
she said. She closed up the
hole and attached the clip.
"You'll be okay now!"
Everyone cheered – everyone except Elliot.
The hole was fixed, but he could barely move his leg.
He couldn't imagine ever having fun again.

Elliot desperately wanted to cry. He longed to be alone.

Socks could see that something was still wrong.

"Elliot needs to rest now," she announced. She pulled out her favourite blanket. The others tiptoed away.

As she tucked him in, Socks noticed the thread still dangling from Elliot's messy leg.

"Hmmm," she murmured. She gave him a pat, then crept softly to the kitchen.

At last Elliot could cry.
With each peek at his leg he
sobbed harder, until finally,
he wore himself out. Elliot
was just drifting off to sleep when he heard something.
He looked up.

Socks was back, with Beaverton.

"Let's see," said Beaverton kindly. He inspected the
damaged leg. Then he picked up the thread.

"Gracious," he chuckled. "Thank goodness Socks
came to get me."

"Hop on my tail," said Beaverton, "I'll give you a lift to my spot. We'll take that stuff off."

"Won't I come apart?" asked Elliot.

"Don't worry. I know how to fix things," Beaverton said proudly.

In the kitchen, Beaverton dug through his cupboard and found a needle and thread. He undid the clip and sponged off the glue. He removed the bandage, the tape and the pin.

Then Beaverton carefully sewed Elliot's leg back together. And he showed Elliot how to sew, too.

"For next time," he said.

Elliot jumped up with relief and ran circles around Socks. He even did cartwheels. He checked his perfect leg again and again. Then he stopped and gave Beaverton a big hug.

"Thank you," he said.

"You're welcome," said Beaverton.

Elliot turned to Socks. But before he could thank her she grabbed his arm.

"Come on, Elliot!" she cheered. "Let's show the others!"

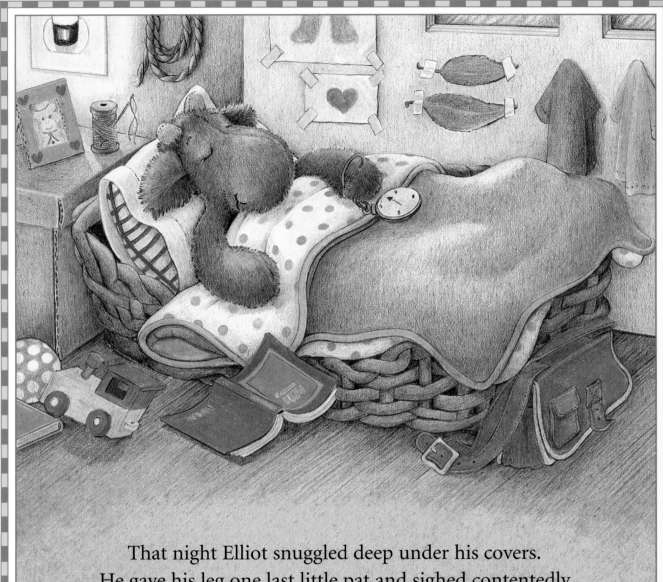

That night Elliot snuggled deep under his covers.
He gave his leg one last little pat and sighed contentedly.
Elliot smiled.
Tomorrow, he and Socks would go exploring.